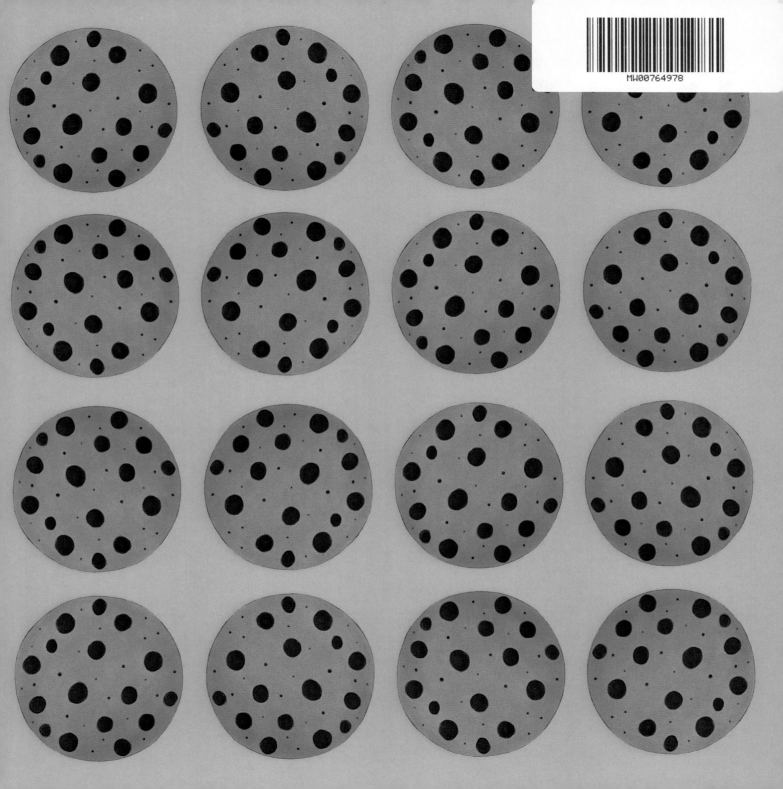

Holly Nichole Zarcone

Copyright © 2017 Holly Nichole Zarcone

ISBN: 1978058357
ISBN-13: 978-1978058354

For my three little monkeys, who I love so much. . .
& who sometimes have cookies for dinner.

ACKNOWLEDGMENTS

Special thanks to my amazing husband for supporting me on this journey. I would also like to thank my forever friend Stacie Mauchan for encouraging me to pick up a pen once more, my Mom and Dad for allowing us to eat that giant slice of chocolate cake for dinner on vacation, and to my children for inspiring me every single day. I also want to thank my incredibly talented illustrator Sophie, who helped bring my words to life.

The day had been long, the weather quite dreary. Mom stood by the sink washing plates that were smear-y. Jack asked for a snack, Cal whined for TV, Dad called to say he's late...

Then Mom looked right at me.

3

She asked if homework was done and if rooms had been cleaned. Were our jackets picked up? Are the costumes cleaned up from last Halloween?

She asked me this and that and about a dozen things more. She asked me about every single, possible chore.

5

She looked at me long and she looked at me hard, her gaze was so stern our dog ran to the yard.

I quietly and quickly said, "Yes, yes, yes, yes." I thought to myself "Boy, my mom's full of stress!" then I scowled and said " We never have fun.", under my breath.

Mom looked at me softer and tears bloomed in her eyes. She looked all around the kitchen and then to my surprise ...She said, "Pull up a chair! Tonight it's cookies for dinner!" I suddenly felt like a lottery winner!

8

9

I looked flabbergasted, Jack's jaw dropped to the floor, Cal threw her hands up. We knew there had to be more.

Could this be a trick?! Are they Brussel sprout cookies?
Or kale, or peas, or the fur from some Wookies?!

Mom gave us each a kiss, a hug, and put out a platter. She had a twinkle in her eye and now we could tell there was nothing the matter. She sat with us smiling wider than we've seen in awhile and we munched and we crunched up the big, giant pile.

12

Mom put on some music and kicked off her shoes, we danced for an hour to some rhythm and blues.

13

The clock ticked past eight and Dad walked through the door. His mouth dropped wide open, as if he could roar. There were cookie crumbs, spilled milk, Mom's hair was askew- I think Jack may have even been missing a shoe! He looked to mom who blew him a kiss; then he shrugged, grabbed a cookie, and was in total bliss.

Mom led a conga line and we got into our beds. Our bellies were full, and so were our heads. Our hearts were so happy as mom flicked off the light, dreams sprung from our minds in our state of delight.

As I closed my eyes and snuggled warm
under my blanket and sheet, I heard Mom
whisper to Dad in a voice so sweet,
"Our kids are kids for only so long, we
must do our best to build them up strong.
Life is so short, we need time to play...
Sometimes cookies for dinner is just the
right way."

About the Author

Holly Nichole Zarcone is a baker turned writer. She lives in New York with her husband and three children. She adores going on adventures with her children, reading, and of course baking the occasional batch of cookies.

About the Illustrator

Sophie Kinsella is an Irish Illustrator who has a degree in Animation after studying for four years at the Dún Laoghaire Institute of Art, Design and Technology in Dublin, Ireland, She now lives in Manhattan New York and is pursuing her career as an Animator while she continues to illustrate on a freelance basis.

Chocolate Chip Cookies for Dinner

Ingredients:

3/4 cup white sugar

1 cup brown sugar

1 cup butter

1 tbsp good quality vanilla

2 large eggs

3 cups all-purpose flour

3/4 tsp baking soda

3/4 teaspoon salt

3 cups semi-sweet chocolate chips

Directions:

Preheat oven to 350 degrees

Cream sugars and butter.

Beat in vanilla and eggs, one at a time.

Combine all dry ingredients and slowly add to wet mixture.

Mix in chocolate chips.

Spoon 1 1/4" balls of dough onto cookie sheets about 2" apart.

Bake 10-12 minutes. Let cool & enjoy!